Scarlett
the Garnet
Fairy

To Josephine Scarlet Whitehouse
— a little jewel, herself

Special thanks to
Sue Mongredien

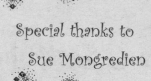

No part of this work may be reproduced, stored in a retrieval system, or transmitted in any form or by any means, electronic, mechanical, photocopying, recording, or otherwise, without written permission of the publisher. For information regarding permission, write to Working Partners Limited, 1 Albion Place, London, W6 0QT, United Kingdom.

ISBN-10: 0-545-01189-2
ISBN-13: 978-0-545-01189-1

20 19 18 17 16 15 14   12/0

Printed in the U.S.A.   40

Scarlett
the Garnet
Fairy

by Daisy Meadows
illustrated by Georgie Ripper

SCHOLASTIC INC.

New York   Toronto   London   Auckland   Sydney
Mexico City   New Delhi   Hong Kong   Buenos Aires

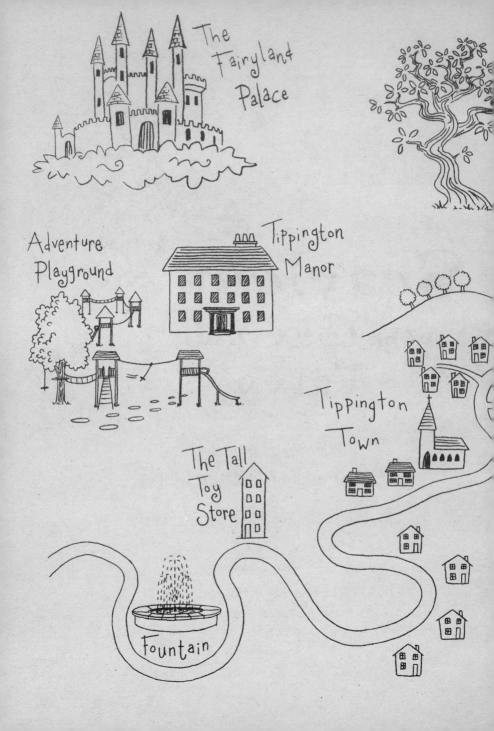

The Fairyland Palace

Adventure Playground

Tippington Manor

Tippington Town

The Tall Toy Store

Fountain

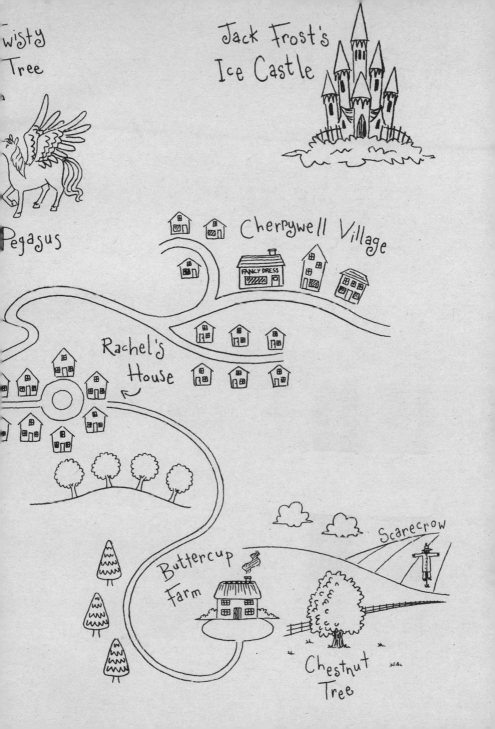

By frosty magic I cast away
These seven jewels with their fiery rays,
So their magic powers will not be felt
And my icy castle shall not melt.

The fairies may search high and low
To find the gems and take them home.
But I will send my goblin guards
To make the fairies' mission hard.

Contents

A Walk on the Farm

"Time to get up!" Rachel Walker called, bouncing on the end of her friend Kirsty's bed. Kirsty Tate was staying with the Walker family during their school break, and Rachel didn't want to waste a single second.

Kirsty yawned and stretched. "I just had the best dream," she said sleepily.

"Queen Titania asked us to help the
Jewel Fairies find seven stolen gemstones
from her magic crown, and . . ." Her
voice trailed away and she opened
her eyes wide. "It wasn't a dream, was
it?" she said, sitting up in bed. "We
really *did* meet India the Moonstone
Fairy yesterday!"

Rachel nodded, smiling. "Yes, we did,"
she agreed.

Kirsty and Rachel shared a wonderful secret. They were friends with the fairies! They had had all sorts of wonderful adventures with them in the past — but now the fairies were in trouble.

Mean Jack Frost had stolen the seven magical jewels from the Fairy Queen's crown. He had tried to keep the jewels for himself, but their magic was so powerful that his ice castle had started to melt. In a rage, Jack Frost had thrown the jewels far away into the human world. Now they were lost.

King Oberon and Queen Titania had asked Rachel and Kirsty to help return the jewels to Fairyland. The day before, the girls had helped India the Moonstone Fairy find the magic moonstone. But there were still six jewels left to find!

"I'm glad the moonstone is safely back in Fairyland," Rachel said. "And I had a great dream last night, so we know for sure that India's dream magic is working again."

The Fairy King and Queen had told the girls all about the jewels from Queen Titania's crown. They controlled some of the most important kinds of fairy magic. Every year, in a special ceremony, the fairies would recharge their magic by dipping their wands in the magical rainbow that streamed from the crown. But Jack Frost had stolen the jewels right before this year's ceremony. And that meant all the fairies were running low on a lot of their special magic.

"We have to track down the other

jewels before the fairies' magic is gone,"
Kirsty said, getting dressed quickly.
"Maybe we'll find another jewel today!"

Rachel agreed, and together the girls
hurried downstairs for breakfast.
Unfortunately, it
drizzled all morning.
There was no sign of
any jewels or any
fairies! After lunch,
though, the clouds
cleared to reveal a
blue sky and sunshine.

"Who wants to
come with me to Buttercup Farm?" Mrs.
Walker asked, clearing the lunch table.
"We need some vegetables and
eggs — and you two look like you could
use some fresh air."

"We could!" Rachel agreed, grinning at Kirsty. She held up crossed fingers while her mom wasn't looking. "Maybe we'll find another jewel," she added in a whisper.

A few minutes later, the girls and Mrs. Walker headed down the street toward the farm. Buttons, the Walkers' dog, trotted happily alongside them, sniffing

at interesting smells on the side of
the road.

"He loves going to the
farm," Rachel told
Kirsty, patting
Buttons. "He's
known the
Johnsons'
sheepdog,
Cloud, since
they were
both
puppies. The
two of them go
crazy whenever
they see each other. Don't you, boy?"

Woof! barked Buttons, as if he agreed
with her.

As the girls walked behind Mrs. Walker, something caught Kirsty's eye. "Look at those," she said, pointing to some red-and-white toadstools under a nearby tree. "They're exactly like the Fairyland toadstool houses, aren't they?" Rachel nodded. "Oh, I hope we meet another fairy today, Kirsty!" she said.

Kirsty crunched through the fallen leaves. "You know what Queen Titania always says," she whispered as Mrs. Walker bent down and let Buttons off his leash. "Don't go looking for magic . . ."

"It will find you!" Rachel finished.

Kirsty linked her arm through Rachel's. "It is hard not to look, though," she confessed. "I keep wondering where we're going to meet our next fairy — and who it's going to be!"

"Here we are," Mrs. Walker said as they turned onto a long driveway.

An old stone farmhouse stood up ahead. It had a pretty thatched roof and smoke curling from the chimney.

A smiling woman opened the front door. "Hello," she called warmly. "Come in, all of you. Oh, Buttons, too! Cloud will be so happy to see him."

"This is my friend Kirsty. She's staying with us," Rachel said. "And Kirsty, this is Mrs. Johnson."

"Hello," Kirsty said, returning Mrs. Johnson's smile.

"Nice to meet you, Kirsty," Mrs. Johnson said, leading the way into the sunny farmhouse kitchen. "I just picked the last few plums from my plum tree. Would anyone like one?"

"Yes, please!" the girls replied.

A chorus of barks greeted them in the kitchen. Cloud, a black-and-white sheepdog, danced around their legs. Buttons ran joyfully after him, barking just as loudly.

"Should we take the dogs for a walk?" Rachel offered as Buttons's tail almost knocked over a basket of eggs.

"Good idea," Mrs. Johnson replied,
 giving each girl a
handful of plums.
"Oh!" she added as
they were about
to head out the
door. "I should
warn you that Mr.
Johnson is in a pretty bad mood. His new
tractor disappeared, and he thinks one of
the farm boys took it for a ride." She
winked at the girls. "So if you see him
and he seems grumpy, don't take it
personally."

The girls nodded and followed
Buttons and Cloud out into the meadow.
Suddenly, Cloud trotted back over to
the girls, looking very pleased with

himself. He dropped something at their feet.

"What's this?" Kirsty asked, bending to pick it up. "Oh, look, Rachel!" she said. "It's a tiny toy tractor." She giggled. "Do you think we should give it to Mr. Johnson to make up for the one he lost?"

Rachel grinned. "I don't think he'd appreciate that," she replied. "We'd better leave it here, in case somebody comes back for it."

Kirsty put the tractor down on a flat patch of grass where it was easy to spot. As she straightened up, she noticed some strange-looking shiny stones. "Are those rocks over there?" she asked.

Rachel turned and looked where her friend was pointing. She saw a few big brown objects under the chestnut tree on one side of the meadow. "That's funny," she said, frowning. "I've never noticed those before. Let's go and take a closer look."

Kirsty and Rachel ran over to

the tree. The things that Kirsty had
spotted were about the size and shape of
soccer balls. They were a glossy
chocolate brown color.
"Well, they're not
rocks," Kirsty
said, touching
one of them.
It felt cool
and smooth
under her
hand. "They
look more like . . . giant chestnuts!"

Rachel touched one, too. "They *do*
look like chestnuts," she agreed. "But
whoever heard of a chestnut this big?"

Before Kirsty could reply, Buttons
bounded over, barking excitedly.

Then he ran back to a patch of grass

a few feet away, sniffed it eagerly, and
barked again.

Rachel went to see what he'd found.
"Kirsty, quick!" she called, her eyes wide.
"Come and look at these sheep!"

"Sheep?" echoed Kirsty, running over
to join her friend. She couldn't see any
sheep, but as she got closer to her friend
she heard a tiny but clear *Ba-a-a-a!*

Rachel pointed down at the grass and
Kirsty looked down, too.

"Tiny sheep!" Kirsty gasped in surprise.
"Oh, wow! Are they real?"

Down by their feet was a flock of the
tiniest sheep Kirsty and Rachel had ever
seen. Sheep the size of mice! Chestnuts
the size of soccer balls! What was
going on?

Rachel's eyes were bright. "There is definitely magic in the air today," she breathed.

"There must be another magic jewel nearby," Kirsty added, feeling a thrill of excitement.

Quickly, the girls put the dogs on their leashes and tied them to the fence, so that the tiny sheep wouldn't accidentally get stepped on.

Just then, Rachel clutched Kirsty's arm. "Kirsty!" she squealed. "Look!"

Both girls stared. A large golden leaf was floating down from the chestnut tree in front of them. And there, sitting on top of it as if she was riding a magic carpet, was a tiny beaming fairy.

Seeing Red

"Wheeeeee!" squealed the fairy
breathlessly. "Hello, girls!"

Kirsty and Rachel laughed as the
golden leaf sailed down to the ground.
The fairy jumped off and twirled up
into the air, her wings beating so quickly
they were a blur of glittering colors. She
had wavy dark brown hair, and wore a

scarlet dress decorated with a pretty
flower. She also wore little, glittery red
shoes that twinkled in the sunlight.

"It's Scarlett the Garnet Fairy," Rachel
cried, recognizing her right away.
"Hello, Scarlett!"

"Of course!" Kirsty said, as she remembered something King Oberon had told them. "The garnet controls growing and shrinking magic!" she exclaimed. "That's why the chestnuts are so huge. . . ."

"And the sheep are so tiny," Rachel added with a smile.

"Exactly," Scarlett said. She waved her wand hopefully, but only a few red sparkles scattered from it. They fizzled and sputtered out in the grass. "And unfortunately, without the garnet, I don't have enough magic to turn things back to their proper sizes. We have to find the

garnet before it
changes anything
else."

She flew over to
perch on Kirsty's
shoulder. "India
told me that you
had a run-in with
Jack Frost's goblins
yesterday," she said,
shivering at the thought. "Let's try and
find the garnet before any goblins show
up today!"

"We'll start right away," Rachel said,
and Kirsty nodded.

"Great," Scarlett replied, smiling. "I'll
check the vegetable patch over there."

"And we'll search this field," Kirsty
said. "Come on, Rachel."

The girls walked slowly across the meadow, scanning the grass for any sign of the garnet. They were just passing a haystack when something very strange happened.

"My legs are tingling!" Kirsty gasped.

"We're shrinking!" Rachel cried as she saw the ground rushing toward her.

The girls had been fairy-size before, but then they'd always had pretty wings to fly with, too! Not this time. They had simply shrunk! Suddenly the haystack seemed like a mountain in front of them, and the grass was waist-high.

"The garnet must be very close, if the magic is working on us now," Kirsty pointed out.

"Scarlett! Hey, Scarlett!" Rachel shouted, trying to attract the fairy's attention. But her voice had shrunk, too. Scarlett couldn't hear her tiny call. "Rachel, look at the

top of the haystack," Kirsty cried,
pointing upward. "It's glowing red!"

Rachel peered up at the haystack, and
sure enough, something at the top was
shining a deep red color. "It must be the
garnet!" she declared. "Let's climb up
and get it for Scarlett."

"Good idea," Kirsty agreed.

The two girls began to climb the haystack. It was very hard work! The hay was sharp and slippery, and it was difficult to get a grip on the smooth stalks. Little by little, the girls drew closer to the magic garnet.

Just as Kirsty was about to reach the top, the piece of hay that she was holding on to suddenly swayed and bent. Kirsty clutched at another stalk, but it snapped in two! "Help!" she cried, desperately trying to hang on. "I'm falling!"

A Scary Surprise

"Here!" Rachel yelled, leaning down to reach Kirsty. "Grab my hand!"

Kirsty clung onto her friend's outstretched fingers, her heart pounding. "Thanks," she said shakily as her feet found a strong straw and Rachel helped pull her back up.

The girls climbed carefully up to the top. Then Rachel gave a triumphant cry. "We found it!" she cheered. In front of them lay the glittering red garnet. The sun shone through it, casting a rich, rosy light across the hay.

"Wow!" breathed Kirsty. The jewel

seemed even more
impressive now
that the girls were
fairy-size. It was
no bigger than a
hen's egg, but
right now that
was almost as
tall as Rachel
and Kirsty!

"Scarlett!" both girls
shouted. They waved their arms around
at the top of the haystack, hoping the
fairy would see or hear them.

But Scarlett was still searching in the
vegetable patch. She had no idea that
her jewel had been found.

Then Kirsty had an idea. "What if we
turn the garnet around so that its red

light shines over to Scarlett?" she suggested. "That will get her attention."

"Perfect!" Rachel agreed. "I bet it's heavy, though. I think we'll have to lift it together."

Kirsty took hold of one side of the jewel, and Rachel held the other. Then Kirsty counted, "One . . . two . . . three!" Together, the girls turned the garnet so that its rosy light was shining right at Scarlett.

The little fairy turned around. When

she saw the girls with the
garnet, her face lit up.
"Hooray!" she cried,
leaping into the air
and twirling for joy.
"You found it!"
Kirsty and Rachel
both took a hand off
the jewel to
wave at her.
When they did,
the garnet
slipped slightly.
Its sparkling red
light danced
farther down
the vegetable
patch, flickering over
a nearby scarecrow.

35

And then, to the girls' surprise, the scarecrow moved!

Rachel and Kirsty stared in amazement as the scarecrow jumped down from its wooden stand and started lumbering its way toward the haystack.

"What's happening?" Rachel asked. "Do you think it's more fairy magic?"

"I don't know," Kirsty replied. "I didn't think the garnet could do that." She watched the scarecrow walking jerkily toward them and suddenly felt nervous. "It's coming this way. What do you think it wants?"

Rachel narrowed her eyes and stared hard at the scarecrow. "Hang on a minute," she said. "Look at its green, pointy nose. That's not a scarecrow — it's a goblin!"

"Oh, no!" Kirsty cried, grabbing Rachel's arm in fright. "Look at how big it is!"

"It's as big as a grown-up," Rachel said anxiously, biting her lip. All of a sudden, she felt smaller than ever. How would she and Kirsty protect the garnet? They were so tiny, and the goblin was so huge! "Oh, hurry up, Scarlett! Come and get the garnet!" she yelled.

Scarlett was flying over as fast as she could, a determined look on her face. "I'm coming," she cried. "Hang on, girls!"

Kirsty gulped, still holding onto Rachel. "Look!" she said, pointing at the scarecrow.

It had stopped walking and was pulling off its long coat. And underneath the coat, there wasn't just one goblin, there were two. One was standing on the other's shoulders! The top goblin jumped down. As Rachel and Kirsty watched in horror, both goblins started running as fast as they could toward the garnet — and the girls.

Kidnapped!

"Let's get out of here," Kirsty cried. She and Rachel began to clamber back down the haystack as quickly as they could, carrying the garnet between them. The jewel felt strangely warm in their hands.

"My fingers are tingling," Rachel called out. "Do you think that means — ?"

But Rachel's words were cut off. The garnet's magic was working again — and this time, both girls were *growing*. They clung tightly to the jewel as their legs lengthened, and their heads moved up toward the sky. Suddenly, the haystack, which had seemed like such a mountain to climb, was nothing more than a regular haystack. It couldn't hold the weight of the two girls! "I'm sinking," Rachel panted as her feet sunk into the hay. "We're too heavy for the haystack now."

Scarlett arrived at that moment, looking anxious. "I'll try to use my magic to get you out of there!" she cried, waving her wand quickly. But only one glittering red sparkle fell out. It fizzled uselessly on the grass. "Oh, no, here come the goblins!" she cried, fluttering protectively in front of Kirsty and Rachel.

"Oh, dear! Oh, dear!" chuckled the taller goblin. He watched as the girls floundered around in the waist-deep hay.

The other, shorter goblin was close behind. "I think we'll take that garnet, thank you very much," he declared, reaching out to snatch it from Rachel's hand.

"Oh, no you don't!" Rachel cried, throwing the precious stone into the air before the goblin could grab it. "Catch, Scarlett!"

Scarlett caught the garnet just in time but, in the human world, it was too big and heavy for her to fly with. She quickly sunk down through the air under the weight of the jewel, flapping her wings as hard as she could to keep from falling too far.

Kirsty could see that Scarlett was trying

to angle her wand so it would touch
the stone. The little fairy was trying
to recharge her wand with growing
and shrinking magic! But before she
could do that, poor Scarlett lost her
grip on the wand. It tumbled down
into the hay.

Luckily, Kirsty pounced
on the wand before
either of the
goblins could
reach it. Then
something
terrible
happened. The
shorter goblin whipped off his scarecrow
hat and held it out under the falling
fairy.

"Help!" Scarlett cried as she plunged helplessly into the dark hat.

"Gotcha!" cheered the goblin. "A garnet *and* a fairy — that's a bonus!"

"Hey!" called Rachel, kicking the hay in an attempt to get out of it. "Let Scarlett go, right now!"

"No way!" Both goblins laughed nastily — and ran away.

As the two girls finally scrambled out of the haystack, the goblins sprinted across the field with Scarlett and the garnet still trapped inside the scarecrow hat. Scarlett couldn't fly out because the goblin held the opening of the hat shut! Kirsty and Rachel could hear the goblins singing happily.

"Twinkle, twinkle, garnet stone,
You are never going home.
Jack Frost wants you hidden away.
Out of Fairyland you'll stay.
Sparkle, sparkle, on and on
The fairies' magic will soon be gone!"

"Come back!" shouted Kirsty angrily.
"Rachel, we have to get that scarecrow
hat . . . before it's too late!"

Dogs to the Rescue

As Rachel and Kirsty took off after the goblins, they looked around for anything that could help them rescue Scarlett. Then Kirsty's gaze fell on Cloud and Buttons. She remembered that, in the past, the goblins had been scared of dogs. "Wait!" she called to Rachel, thinking

fast. "Maybe Buttons and Cloud can help us!"

It seemed like the dogs had already had the same idea. They were both pulling on their leashes and barking at the goblins.

"Come on, boy," Rachel said, letting Buttons off his leash. "Let's go goblin catching!"

"You too, Cloud," Kirsty said, unclipping his leash. "Go, dogs, go!" Cloud and Buttons did not need to be told twice. With a loud chorus of barks, they both ran eagerly toward the goblins.

The goblin carrying the scarecrow hat looked back over his shoulder and screeched with fear when he saw the dogs. "Quick!" he yelled to his friend. "Climb on top of the scarecrow stand!"

Both goblins scrambled back up the wooden stand. They clung tightly to its beams.

Woof! Woof! Woof! Buttons and Cloud barked happily, jumping up and trying to lick the goblins' toes.

"Eek!" yelped the tall goblin, pulling his feet up. "Go away, you horrible mutts!"

Kirsty and Rachel ran over. "This is all your fault," they heard the tall goblin hiss at his friend. "It was your idea to climb up here!"

"Well, if you ran faster we could have been out of here by now," the short one moaned back.

"Is everything OK?" Kirsty asked sweetly. She patted Cloud and Buttons, who were still looking up hopefully at the goblins. They wanted to play!

"No!" snapped the tall goblin.

"Just send the dogs away!" the short goblin begged.

"I don't think so," Rachel replied cheerfully. "Unless . . ."

"What? What?" the goblins cried together.

"Unless you set Scarlett free," Kirsty finished.

The short goblin looked thoughtful and scratched his leathery green head. "All right," he said at last. "The fairy can go. But the garnet is staying right here, in my hat."

"OK," the girls agreed.

Rachel grabbed both dogs by their collars and held them back. "Now, let Scarlett go," she said.

The goblin carefully opened the

hat just wide enough for Scarlett to
flutter out.

She zoomed through the gap and flew
over to land on Kirsty's shoulder. "Thank
you," she said as Kirsty
handed her wand back.
"That hat smelled
awful!"

"Well, you're still not
getting your hands on
our jewel," the goblin said,
reaching into the hat to pat the garnet.
"You might as well — hey!" he suddenly
yelped in surprise. "What's happening?"

Kirsty, Rachel, and Scarlett stared at
the goblin. And then all three of them
began to laugh.

"It's the garnet!" Scarlett laughed. "It's
making him shrink!"

Sure enough, the short goblin was growing even shorter before their eyes. "Help! Make it stop!" he squeaked in a tiny voice.

His friend was chuckling loudly — but not for long. Now that there was one big goblin and one tiny goblin on the scarecrow's stand, the whole thing was off balance.

"*Whoa!*" the big goblin cried as he began to fall. "Help!"

Goblins on the Run

Splat!

The girls backed out of the way just as the large goblin landed on the ground. "Oof!" he panted. "Stupid garnet!"

Woof! barked the dogs, running over and licking the goblin playfully.

Woof! Woof!

Rachel and Kirsty couldn't help smiling

as the goblin rolled around, helpless with
laughter. "It tickles!" he roared. "Ooh, it
tickles!"

Then Kirsty remembered the garnet.
She rushed over to the scarecrow pole
where the tiny goblin was still hanging
on. Kirsty plucked the hat easily from
his arms.

"Hooray!" cheered Scarlett when she saw the magic garnet gleaming in Kirsty's hand. "Great job, Kirsty!"

"We did it!" Rachel cried. "We found another jewel."

The girls and Scarlett headed back toward the farmhouse. They called the dogs to follow them, once they were a safe distance from the goblins.

Then Scarlett carefully touched her wand to the magic garnet and waved it in the air. A stream of glittering red fairy dust flooded out across the fields. A smile lit up Scarlett's face. "That's more like it!" she said.

Baa! Baa! The sheep were suddenly back to their normal size. Cloud and Buttons stared at them in confusion, wondering where they had come from.

Cloud sniffed at a stray red sparkle and
jumped as it fizzed into thin air under
his nose.

Kirsty turned to look at the chestnut tree.
The giant chestnuts had disappeared. They
had shrunk to their normal size again! And
what was that, in the middle of the field?

"Mr. Johnson's tractor!" Rachel laughed.
"The garnet must have shrunk that, too.
Remember, we thought it was a toy?"

Kirsty grinned as the last few bright
twinkles of fairy magic disappeared from

the tractor's wheels. "Now Mr. Johnson will be in a good mood again," she said happily.

"And so will King Oberon and Queen Titania when I send this garnet back to Fairyland," Scarlett added.

The tiny goblin had been turned back to his regular size, too. The girls and Scarlett watched as he jumped down from the wooden stand and stomped away with his goblin friend. Although the girls couldn't hear what they were saying, it was clear that they were arguing again.

Scarlett chuckled. "And that's the last

we'll see of them," she said,
sounding satisfied. She
touched her wand to the
garnet once more and it
vanished in a fountain of
glittering red fairy dust.

"Now the garnet is
safely back in Fairyland,"
Rachel said with a sigh of
relief. The air where the garnet had been
shimmered for a second, then returned to
normal.

"And I should be going back, too,"
Scarlett added, hugging the girls good-
bye. "Thank you for all your help, Kirsty
and Rachel. And good luck finding the
other magic jewels!"

The girls waved as the tiny fairy
zoomed away to Fairyland.

"Phew," Rachel said as they headed back to the farmhouse. "That was close. For a minute, I thought the goblins were going to get away with the garnet *and* Scarlett."

Kirsty ruffled Cloud's shaggy coat. "Well, thanks to these two dogs, both Scarlett and the garnet are safe and sound," she declared with a smile.

Rachel grinned at Kirsty. "Come on," she said, breaking into a run. "We'll have more fairy adventures soon, but for now, I'm starving. I wonder if Mrs. Johnson has any more of those plums left."

"I hope so," Kirsty said, running after her friend. "Race you there!"

The Jewel Fairies

India and Scarlett both have their magic
jewels back. Can Rachel and Kirsty help

Emily the
Emerald Fairy?

Toy Trouble

"Wow!" Kirsty Tate gasped, her eyes wide with amazement. "This is the biggest toy store I've ever seen!"

Her best friend, Rachel Walker, laughed. "I know," she agreed. "Isn't it great?"

Kirsty nodded. Wherever she turned, there was something wonderful to see. In one corner of the toy store was a huge display of dolls in every shape and size, along with an amazing number of dollhouses. A special, roped-off area was filled with remote-control cars, buses, trucks, and airplanes. Nearby stood rows of bikes, skateboards, and scooters.

Shelves were piled high with every board game Kirsty could think of, plus stacks of computer games. Colorful kites hung from the ceiling, along with big balloons and spinning mobiles. Kirsty had never seen anything like it, and this was only the first floor!

"Look over there, Kirsty," Rachel said, pointing at the dolls.

Kirsty saw a sign that read MEET FAIRY FLORENCE AND HER FRIENDS. She stared at the dolls displayed around the sign. Fairy Florence wore a long pink dress. She looked boring and old-fashioned. Kirsty and Rachel glanced at each other and burst out laughing.

"Fairy Florence doesn't look like a real fairy at all!" Rachel whispered, and Kirsty nodded.

Rachel and Kirsty knew what real fairies looked like because they'd met them . . . many times! The two girls had often visited Fairyland to help their fairy friends when they were in trouble. Maybe they would have another fairy adventure today!

When the grown-ups are clueless, these kids save the day!

There are some pretty weird grown-ups living in Bailey City. Meet them all in this wacky adventure series!

A JIGSAW JONES MYSTERY®

Elementary, my dear Mila. Jigsaw Jones is the *best* detective in the second grade!

Available wherever you buy books.
www.scholastic.com/kids

LITTLE APPLE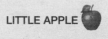

SCHOLASTIC

FILLLA3

A fairy for every day!

The seven Rainbow Fairies are missing! Help rescue the fairies and bring the sparkle back to Fairyland.

When mean Jack Frost steals the Weather Fairies' magical feathers, the weather turns wacky. It's up to the Weather Fairies to fix it!

Jack Frost is causing trouble in Fairyland again! This time he's stolen the seven crown jewels. Without them, the magic in Fairyland is fading fast!

Look for The Pet Fairies— Coming soon!

SCHOLASTIC

www.scholastic.com

FAIRY